Wildest Dreams

By Michael Young

Edited by Dominique Lambright

ROYAL MEDIA
AND PUBLISHING LLC

Royal Media and Publishing

P. O. Box 4321

Jeffersonville, IN 47131

502-802-5385

http://royamediaandpublishing.com

royalmediapublishing@gmail.com

Cover Design: Gad Savage – Elite Covers

ISBN-13: 978-0-9987154-4-5

Printed in the United States of America

Dedication

This book is dedicated to my grandmother Virginia Young who sparked my love of books.

Acknowledgements

I wish to acknowledge my fans for encouraging and supporting me as I bring them original and unique story telling.

Michael A. Young

Table of Contents

Dedication		ii
Acknowledgements		v
Introduction		vii
Chapter 1	Falling Star	1
Chapter 2	Time For Something New	9
Chapter 3	Unbelievable Encounter	17
Chapter 4	Flirting or Flaunting	27
Chapter 5	Things Just Got Real	37
Chapter 6	What I Need vs What I Want	49
Chapter 7	Neglecting Responsibilities	65
Chapter 8	Life of A Star	71

Chapter 9	Fed Up	83
Chapter 10	Is that Really You?!	95
Chapter 11	Open or Closed	103
Chapter 12	I Put My Name on It	111
Chapter 13	Trouble Finds a Way	121
Chapter 14	I Never Knew	129
Epilogue		135

Introduction

It will be said several times in your life. Sometimes sarcastically, and other times in question form, but no matter how you say it you never really expect it to come true. The phrase… "In your Wildest Dreams." For a minute just think about this, what if your Wildest Dreams came true? What if the unimaginable became imaginable? Something you never thought possible actually happened. Win the lottery, have everything in your life go perfectly. Or how about meeting your favorite celebrity. Better than that, how about your favorite celeb wanting you. Wanting to have sex with you. Wanting to love you.

Or would the undeniable love of an ordinary woman be enough compared to the hope of love returned. Ask yourself would you go with ordinary everyday love or would you go with living the high life and all that comes with it, just to hope your love is returned? What if you had the chance to have it answered? What if you could have your Wildest Dreams?

Wildest Dreams

Chapter 1
Falling Star

First it was the clang of ice falling into a cup, followed by the pouring of a warm liquid, which made the ice pop and crack. Beautiful dark red lips part letting the freshly chilled beverage glide over the tongue then down her throat. Sitting the now empty glass down it was quickly refilled, drank, refilled, and drank repeatedly. After about five or six refills the glass is finally sat down to stay. Walking away from the kitchen counter the woman strolls into another room letting her hips swing. She sat down in a lovely plush chair in front of a glass door that was partially open. A warm night breeze blew her hair and caressed her face, putting a small, very small smile on her face. She got up and went to the sliding door to open it all the way so she could step outside and enjoy her view of the city from the hillside balcony. Looking to the left and right there were no neighbors outside enjoying the night air. Her eyes darted around not focusing on anything in particular. Then the tears started, and they came large and uncontrollable. Almost buckling and falling to her knees she goes back in and slams the door behind her. Dropping down in the chair the woman replayed the events of earlier that night.

Sitting in a dark theatre amongst a nice size crowd of people they all watched an early showing of a soon to be released movie by T'ondra Dove. Dove…used to be a big-ticket drawer, but lately as in the last four or five years her movies haven't been doing too well at the box office. For a brief time, her manager thought that straight to DVD movies would cause a resurgence in her popularity. The paychecks weren't as big as feature film, but they kept her bank account full. They mainly cast her in foolish and very low range roles. Nothing like the leading actress roles from years past. Then this script came along, it was supposed to be her come back into the spotlight role. She had always been cast in the comedy roles, but what the public didn't really know was T'ondra was actually a silly woman. Her roles never let her be herself, just that over the top hyper chick or oblivious pretty woman. This new movie, this new script, was putting her in unfamiliar waters. A serious character with more than one emotion.

As the movie played, some people in the crowd laughed at moments that were supposed to be tear jerkers. Giggled when she was being dead serious delivering a line. What hurt was when quite a few people got up and left midway through the movie saying out loud, "This is the biggest and worst piece of shit that has ever been made." When the film finally ended, she hoped just a few would applaud or cheer. Sitting in disguise along with the director she waited, then finally got a reaction from the audience. Boos mixed with uncontrollable laughter. Getting up with some of the people around her she quickly headed to the exit. Completely embarrassed T'ondra damn near ran out of the cinema, but waiting outside was reporters drooling to interview her because they had already got word from early exiters that this movie wasn't a bomb. It was a grade A nuclear weapon of destruction.

"Ms. Dove, Ms. Dove! Do you have a comment on what people are saying about this movie? That this is finally the film that finishes off your career?"

Not giving a response, or even looking at a camera or outstretched microphone in her path, she made her way to a limo that was waiting out front. Jumping in, or in better words, diving in she tells the driver to get in and take her home as fast as possible. Once home she heads right to her stash of liquor. Not the high dollar for show in a cabinet liquor. She opens the everyman everyday bourbon and sits on a stool. The first taste went down straight out the bottle, then came the glass.

Getting back up from the stool and starting to feel the numbing effects of the many drinks, she goes back to the counter where she was drinking to answer her cell phone that has been ringing and vibrating nonstop for some time now. No one would call this often this time of night except 1 person. Danny Meek. Danny is her long-time manager. He was with her when she was on top of the world. From back when she was basically just a model attempting to be an actress, until she became one of the best-paid women in comedy films. Through her downward spiral of bad film after bad film. True enough, some of those movies were just to pay the bills, but a couple weren't bad movies, they just didn't bring in the money the studios thought they should. Danny stayed loyal to her and she to him.

With a mix of crying and drunkenness she answered the phone. "Hello Danny. The movie fuckin' bombed with the audience. Some got up and left, some laughed. Worse than that they even booed. They booed me! They booed; this was my first role in a serious film and they did that shit!"

"Calm down T'ondra. Maybe it was just a bad crowd."

"No, it wasn't just a bad crowd. It's another bad movie. My career is a piece of shit now and it just got flushed."

"It's not that bad. T'ondra Dove is still a household name. People are used to seeing you in funny roles. Give them time to see your true range. You have had a run of bad breaks in roles and I take full blame for those because I sent you the scripts. I won't tell you to call it a career because you still have talent. What I will say is take a break for a while. Let the industry miss you."

"What should I do? I don't have that young fresh face to model anymore. Not to mention my body has aged too."

"Your face and body are fine. How about you use this time and do that remodeling around the house like you wanted."

"I won't be bringing any checks in, so how will I afford to do it. Lord knows this place needs to be refreshed, I can't be wasting money right now."

"Check with Andrea first, but I'm sure your bank account won't take that big of a hit. That's why we suggested you get a nice house instead of one of those huge money draining mansions."

"By the way thank you for that because I would have been up shit creek if I had tried to buy what I wanted at first."

Feeling like her mood is starting to lighten up Danny tells her to forget about earlier and go to bed. Start the day fresh talking with Andrea about a remodeling budget. She said OK and hung up. Thinking of having 1 last drink she decided against it, locked up downstairs, went up to shower, and lied down to go to sleep.

Finally, in bed she thought about all the things she wanted to change. More important than that, she needed to relax, so she opens the drawer in the nightstand and pulls out a vibrator. Saying to herself, "I need to get a good fucking...and soon." After a few minutes with her toy T'ondra finally comes and drifts off to sleep.

Chapter 2

Time For Something New

The next day sometime in the evening T'ondra was finally able to function again. All that drinking the night before gave her a massive headache. After downing a few aspirins, she calls Andrea like her manager suggested. Andrea Koss was her financial advisor and her best friend. They had become friends long before T'ondra became famous. Back when they both would run into each other trying out for the same modeling gigs. Andrea gave up on it and used her degree in finance too much success. She advised T'ondra to put money to the side and not to waste money on a lot of expensive cars because you can only drive 1 at a time. Just get a nice ride and be done with it. It was also suggested that she keep her circle small. Not just friends, but people she could trust because friends can do you worse than an associate would when it comes to money.

"As your advisor and looking at your financial chart, it looks like you have plenty of money to do some renovating. As your longtime friend... girl all you need is some good dick. Some leg cramping, jaws hurting, coochie swollen sex, but since you haven't had a man in your world in a long time, I guess that's out the window. Even that short time you switched up your diet and dated that raggedy tramp Kennetha, at least that was some sex."

Laughing T'ondra tells Andrea, "To hell with you girl. So what, I got down with a girl for a minute. Shit that bitch ate me better than any man ever did. You wanna know what she used to do with her tongue and some ice rings?"

"Fuck no and thank you in advance for sparing me the details."

"On the real if it will lift your spirits go ahead and change up something, but you need a man. Check that. A good man that's not in the industry at all."

"That's true. All these actor guys just think of themselves, like the spotlight is always and only on them."

"How about a regular guy. A 9-5 with a full bank account guy!?"

The two women talked and laughed for a little while longer with T'ondra asking Andrea to find a good contractor for her and if at all possible, let him be attractive. Nothing would be worse than having an ugly fat man in her house for hours at a time, weeks to a couple months. Andrea said she would do what the budget would allow, but with no promises she would try to find something sexy.

Far across town in the not so great part of town an elderly man and his equally aged wife stood in front of their home almost in tears as they were led around the property by a tall muscular man in a shirt and tie. This may seem like a couple looking over a home before the bank foreclosed on it, but it was nothing like that. The couple had decided to use most of the money saved in a life savings to remodel the house. The kids were grown, moved out, and had families of their own, so spending money to spruce things up was acceptable considering they were in their golden years. What actually made them cry was that everything asked for was done to such perfection and beauty it was amazing. Plus, the contractor did it all under budget. Secretly it wasn't under budget, but he used some of his own money, so they wouldn't drain the saving they were using. The couple was so nice and sweet he had to help them out. Not that he overcharges his clients, but on rare occasions he would go into his own pocket.

"Oh my God! The house looks wonderful. The yard is manicured with a brick path going around plus a flower bed and fountain for Ruby. A new deck with a swing, fresh paint." The elderly man said to the contractor as he held his hand shaking it.

"Don't forget we finally have that white picket fence you been trying to finish for 15 years Larry!"

"Son you did all this with that meager amount of money we gave you. Sir you are just a blessing. We have to owe more for all this."

"Mr. Maze not only did you give me enough to do everything, but I also have a little envelope here for you to put back in your savings."

As he tried to give them the envelope Mrs. Maze touched his hand with her frail hand and told him to keep it as a tip for making an old couples dream come true. He dared not argue with them. He just smiled and said thank you, you two are far too kind. The truth was he used close to $5,000 of his own money and the envelope had about $2,000 in it. He suspected Mr. Maze knew what he had done and that's why he was crying, not because of his yard.

After lots of hugs from Ruby and pats on the back from Larry, the contractor finally got back to his truck. Starting up, waving goodbye, and pulling off. Scott Mozell headed to his office. At a stop light he checked his phone to see the schedule for remaining clients. After a quick once over he saw nothing was on the list. That wasn't good, not that he didn't like the downtime, but he would tend to drink to help forget about the hole in his heart his ex-girlfriend left. No matter how much he drank the pain always came back. The memories always returned, but when he stayed busy, he had no time to think of her. Only time to concentrate on whatever job he was doing. Closing the page on the phone he pulled away and had a sudden thirst for a strong drink. Then the cell rang. It was his partner Daryl Flenn.

Answering he says, "What's good D? Just finished showing the Mazes' what their money bought them."

"That's great Scott. My man have I got a special job for you! You will love me..."

"Who the hell have you signed me up with? Better not be another government job. You know those assholes stiffed us on the bills claiming it was for the benefit of the city."

Laughing, Daryl tells him my bad on those and that he thought high profile clients like that would help the business grow, not put them behind for a while. "Dude I got us a big-name client. A well-known client. Shit...I didn't even know this person had property here…"

"Spit it out man! Who we working for?"

"My friend, my partner, my brother from a father's side chick…I got us an appointment to consult with your dream crush."

"You bullshitting me!"

"No sir. You will be in front of the one and only T'ondra Dove!"

Chapter 3

Unbelievable Encounter

A few days have passed, and Scott has thought of nothing but his upcoming meeting with T'ondra Dove. After watching all her movies to make sure he could handle her beauty properly. The last thing he wanted to do was become a crazed star fan rather than a professional businessman. How would it look for her trying to show him what she wanted to be done and he was just staring at her with his mouth open? The characters she played all seem to be very light-hearted and very fun, but that could be just the characters she played. In reality she could be this queen diva bitch.

His main problem would not only be how attractive she is, but he has seen her semi-naked. In the movies T'ondra either has her breast come out or is walking around in a thong. In his opinion she has a perfect body judging her shape, fullness of titties, the thickness of hips, not to mention that juicy ass. Topping it off would be her perfect skin which could be great makeup or camera work. Whatever the case she was simply the hottest woman that was ever created, and this is why he had to get himself together. How embarrassing would it be to get a hard-on in front of a client.

Scott has worked for some beautiful women since he started his own business, and some went as far to offer themselves for a discount in price. Not that he had overcharged them mind you. They just wanted that hookup deal. Being a professional and a gentleman he never accepted those offers. Tempted though but rejected in the kindest way possible. Now Ms. Dove on the other hand… Scott finally got himself together, took a few deep breaths as he adjusted himself in his boxers and left his home to go see the amazing T'ondra Dove. He said out loud as he got in his consultation car, "Daryl I owe you big for this one partner!"

Steam filled the bathroom as T'ondra readied herself for the consultation with Custom Dreams remodeling company. Andrea said this company came highly recommended with a 97% satisfaction rating. Wanting the best for her friend and client Andrea checked on that 3% dissatisfaction. Turns out it was posted by an elderly woman that claimed the company didn't put a fence back exactly where it was. That was because the city expanded the sidewalk 3 feet into the yards all through the neighborhood. The lady didn't care, she said tear up the sidewalk and put the fence back where it was. So, if that foolishness was the only complaint the company was certainly qualified.

Stepping out of the shower T'ondra heard her cell phone ringing and reached over to pick it up, but it slipped out of her hand. "Damn phone! I really need to get a new case for this thing." Looking at the screen she noticed she has missed seven calls, six from Drea and 1 from someone named Scott

Mozell. A name she didn't recognize so he wouldn't get a callback.

"Hello Drea. My bad on missing your calls I was taking a long shower before the guy comes to give a quote on the remodeling."

"I was calling to see if you were ready. He should be on the way or at least real close because he called me after he said he called you and got no answer."

As she walked into the bedroom letting the towel fall from around her body and putting on a nice t-shirt she says, "Called me? No one called…" then she paused. "What is this guy's name that is coming from the company?"

"He is the owner. Scott Mozell."

"Oh shit. He did call, while I was in the shower. Fuck! About 30 minutes ago. Damn how long was I in there!" Just then the doorbell sounded.

"Girl this man's work is off the chain. You better go answer that door before he leaves and moves someone else in your spot."

"Shit girl. His work and price better be worth your hype."

Hanging up the phone she hurried down to answer the door before it was too late. Not even bothering to look through the peephole or for that matter checking the home security monitors upstairs, she opens the door to see a tall well-built man standing on her front porch. Scott wasn't model quality good looking, but he was handsome. Nicely trimmed, short beard outlined his face with a nearly bald head. Piercing dark brown eyes locked onto her as a smile revealed porcelain white teeth. His mouth began moving, but no sound was heard because her attention was now on his body. A mint green silk shirt and cream-colored tie covered a chest that has definitely seen work in a gym. His biceps threatened to rip through the sleeves as his arms moved upward. Thick thighs filled the cream-colored slacks he wore. Not to mention there seemed to be some muscle behind the zipper that was just as impressive as the other muscles. It didn't bulge or anything, but a woman whose body needs real sexual satisfaction can spot things like that. The icing on this human cake was his mocha complexion.

"Damn!"

Still with a smile Scott said, "Excuse me Ms. Dove. What was that?"

Realizing that comment didn't stay in her head but made it to her mouth she said, "Oh... damn. Damn because I didn't realize it was time for our appointment already. Please forgive me and come inside." She backed up to let him walk inside. Also, she wanted to check out his butt. High and tight...check. Damn was the word again only this time it stayed in her head. Closing the door and walking past him she finally remembered she was wearing only a long t-shirt. Between Andrea on the phone, just getting out the shower and the doorbell ringing she completely forgot to put on the shorts and panties that was laying on the bed. Although the t-shirt wasn't very long, they still covered most of her ass. As she walked toward the kitchen, she noticed him checking her out. Maybe she could work this to her advantage.

"By the way Ms. Dove, my name is Scott Mozell. I am the owner and head foreman for Custom Dreams Remodeling."

"Pleased to meet you Mr. Mozell. Of course, I am....."

"T'ondra Dove. Star of over five major films and co-star in another four movies. Four films where you made a guest appearance, three straight to DVD and one soon to be released movie where you make your dramatic debut."

With a smile spreading across her face she walks behind a small island in the middle of the kitchen and leans forward. "My, my, my, it looks like I have a fan in my presence." She moved behind the counter not because she was ashamed of being half naked, but this Mr. Mozell was making her kitty juicy and it was starting to run down her leg. Like it wasn't bad enough the cool air in the house was making her nipples hard, now she is juicing.

Scott stepped forward against the island himself and placed a large digital pad down in front of her. This was so he could actually begin the consultation and to hide the hard-on he now had from noticing Ms. Dove was wearing no under clothes.

Stay professional Mozell. Stay professional. You have seen her naked ass before, but not in person......damn she is beyond fine. That's what he was telling himself to try and put his man muscle back down.

The two looked over some of his companies' renovations from other projects. From small landscaping to full home makeovers. Everyday homeowners to high-class celebrities. Even a few clients she actually knew, but the funny thing was she thought her friends paid triple the prices he was quoting. Scott smiled and told T'ondra that he wasn't trying to get rich off any client. He just wanted to provide a remodeling plan that exceeded their expectations at a more than fair price. All he asked was that they refer him to any of their friends that was thinking of doing any kind of home changes.

T'ondra wanted to change the whole look and feel of her home. They walked around each room as she pointed out what she had in mind. Scott said nothing as he recorded her words with a mini recorder. He didn't want to put any ideas in her head that would conflict with what she really wanted. This was her vision, he was only there to make it a reality. Before they actually got started T'ondra went and put on some yoga pants but left the undies on the bed on purpose. Thinking why not give a fan a small treat this once.

After the walkthrough was done Mr. Mozell went back to the kitchen island and gave her an estimate. Seeing the price T'ondra did a double take. "This is your estimate? Is this all for everything I want or is this per room?"

"No ma'am. That is a rough quote for the full project. Give or take a few hundred."

"Well Mr. Mozell. You are hired and how soon can you start?"

"Thank you. I can start in 2 days if that is okay with you?"

"That would be fine. I still have to move…"

"Ms. Dove we take care of all that. Like I said we are very professional."

They shook hands and he left out the door. T' went right to her phone to call Andrea to say thank you for recommending Mozell and tell her he was about a 1/2 hour away from being sexed down if he didn't leave when he did. Scott walked to his car adjusting his dick and pulled out his phone to tell Daryl he damn near busted in his boxers from being around Ms. Dove.

Chapter 4
Flirting or Flaunting

It has been a few days now and the remodeling of Ms. Doves' home is well on the way. Furniture in the rooms that are being redone sit in small storage containers in the driveway. Like Mr. Mozell said, his company is very professional. As she walked through her home and looked around, the few workers that were in her home were only concerned with their work. Being extra polite and courteous to her like yes ma'am and announcing themselves before entering a room in which she might be in. Also, they dressed in Polo shirts with the company's name and logo with first names stitched on the chest. The whole situation made her feel at ease. Scott frequently went room to room assisting his men where he needed. Not checking on them, but helping. They were all grown men and didn't want to do anything that would give the company a bad name in which would affect having a good paycheck.

T'ondra had a meeting with Andrea and didn't want to be late for it, so she got dressed quickly to not keep her advisor waiting. She told Scott she had a meeting to attend and would be available if he had any questions. Walking out the side door with a bottle under arm and two glasses in hand T' swung her ass in a playful way to get Andreas attention as she sat on the deck by the pool.

"How is everything going so far girl?"

"They are working their asses off and some of these men have very sweet asses."

"Well hell! Maybe we should be having this wine inside then." Andrea says crossing her legs and pouring a glass of wine for each of them.

The two women continued to talk but were interrupted by Mr. Mozell. He didn't believe the skylight that was about to be put in was going to be in the best possible spot. It was better to have her look and be sure about the location before a hole was cut in the roof, possibly patched up and cut again.

"Hello ladies. I am sorry to interrupt your meeting, but Ms. Dove I would like for you to come and check the placement of the skylight before we cut open your roof please. Best to get it perfect the first time."

"Sure. No problem, we were just having girl talk. Come on Drea, come see EVERYTHING." Then T'ondra gave her a wink and a smile.

After looking in on the work and agreeing with Scott they told him they would be going back out for more wine. As they left out Drea noticed Mr. Mozell checking out their booties, especially T'. Moving close to T' Andrea says, "Let's have some fun. Let's get in the pool."

"Get in the pool?"

"Yes! Get in the pool. These men are too fine and that Mozell is super sexy. Plus, he was checking out our asses. Well yours more than mine, but some attention is better than none."

Looking back over her shoulder she caught him still looking then he turned around and spoke to his men. "Fuck it girl. Why not? I need to have some fun. I got some suits upstairs, one might fit you."

"Bitch so what you got more ass and titties than me. This puss is still knee-buckling good." Drea told T'ondra as she put up the middle finger to her.

While they were upstairs trying on bathing suits Scott called up to T'ondra from the middle of the stairs to tell her that they were done for the day and the men were leaving, but he would still be there 'til after he did his daily after work check.

She told him ok and looked at Andrea. "He will be the only one still here."

Andrea and T'ondra smiled at each other. T' threw the suit she had picked out on the floor. "Two-piece bikini time!"

Drea chose a red bikini with a spaghetti string top and a bottom that only covered half her ass. T'ondra on the other hand chose a white bikini that was basically see through once it got wet. It had a strapless top and a G-string bottom that only covered the lips of her pussy. She was supposed to wear it in a movie, but with her thick figure and the smallness of the bikini all the men couldn't keep their dicks from getting hard. Some even went to jack off after seeing her come out of her trailer, so the outfit went home with her and not put in the movie.

Once they saw the last work truck leave the women came out the bedroom wearing the bikinis being very loud to make sure Scott knew they were still in the house. He heard them coming downstairs, but had his hands full holding a couple buckets full of plaster mix. After he took the remaining tools and buckets out front to his work truck, Scott returned back inside to tell Ms. Dove they were done for the day and her home will be hers alone again till the next morning. Stepping in he called for her, but got no response. As he went further in he could hear the women laughing somewhere out near the patio. Stepping through the sliding door he saw her friend Andrea Koss sitting on the side of the pool with her feet hanging in. As he paid more attention, he noticed she was in a very nice bikini that lifted her breast oh so well and the boy short bottom hugged her brown ass like a baby held a teddy bear. Andrea looked over the top of her sunglasses and saw Mr. Mozell had stopped dead in his tracks admiring her, which would be great, but she already had a man in her life. Not a great man, but a man.

Andrea said softly to herself, "Got 'em!" Then she kicked one foot hard underwater making a big splash. Scott continued to walk over when T'ondra emerged out of the pool next to Andrea. In slow motion she pulled herself out and stood to shake her coal black shoulder-length hair.

His mouth watered as he took her beautiful figure in. Muscular thighs under an ass that looks like two brown sugar bowling balls. Plus, she had on a mother fucking thong… "Oh my damn!" He says under his breath. She wiped her face and turned towards Scott and waved for him to come over. As she waved her titties bounced.

"Oh fuck! I can see her nipples and areola through that top like it's not even there. Holly shit!...I can see the split in her pussy too!"

Scott tried to walk as normal as possible, but his dick was getting harder with each step closer to the women. Then her friend stood up, full hard on now. Scott's a man of integrity and he was not the kind of man that would stand around and just stare at women although he did appreciate the sight of one. So, to stand in front of these two gorgeous women and hold a conversation would in fact be difficult, but not impossible. He told them all that was completed and what else needed to be finished. To not seem like a pervert, he placed his hands in his pockets so he could hide the motion of him pushing his man muscle downward against his leg.

T'ondra knew she got a good stiff reaction from Scott because she saw his hand moving in his pants. Before he left T' mentioned to him about redoing the patio area. She asked Andrea if it could fit into her budget. Drea took a sip of the drink in her hand and told her, "Sure. I think so, just as long as you don't try to make it like something off cribs."

"Great!" T'ondra shouted as she turned to the pool. As she did her left hand went back and grazed Scott's penis. Normally a person would jerk away, but determined to be an over the top flirt right now she kept it there moving it back and forth against his swollen muscle. Feeling it pop out through the hole in his boxers he backs away and says do you mind if I use the restroom before I leave? She says why of course not, you know where it is. After he goes back inside the two women embrace each other and burst out in laughter almost falling in the pool together. T'ondra stops laughing and tells Andrea that she forgot that she has a meeting with Danny in the morning about a small cameo role in an upcoming movie and needs to call him. She walks as fast as she could on the wet pavement to go get her phone in the bedroom.

Inside Scott was in the bathroom readjusting himself. He looked in the mirror and smiled thinking they were flirting with me. Two beautiful woman and one is my ultimate crush. He should have rubbed up against her ass with his hardness, but no. This is a business arrangement not a sexual fantasy. Just then T'ondra came up behind him and called his name startling him. He turned around very quickly with his…man muscle still in hand. T'ondra looked down and saw his long thick chocolate thrill toy in his hand and she felt her knees buckle.

"Oh my God! You are blessed!"

"Excuse me? What was that?" Scott asked smiling while he stuffed himself back in his boxers and zips his pants up.

"Shit I just damn near forgot my own name. Oh yeah. I have a meeting in the morning, could you get here a little earlier or start after I return?"

"No problem. I can do whatever you need. You're the client and I'm here for your needs. I will be here early just let me know what time."

Taking a quick look back down at his crotch then back up to his face she says, "Make it about 7am if you please."

"Yes ma'am. 7am it is." Then he steps past her and tells her good evening.

Feeling her cookie get moist she says under her breath, "Better watch that whatever you need. I just saw something that I may need."

Chapter 5
Things Just Got Real

Danny and T'ondra sat at a corner table in a nice quiet high-class coffee house. Most of the customers were either in line or sitting outside at patio tables sipping coffee, teas, and cappuccinos. Who knows what crazy conversations they were having because all the sounds mixed in were an unrecognizable jumble? Inside though a conversation was very audible and plain, but no one paid any attention. It was in the more as they say a higher class of people with black cards, not basic credit cards. Even though T'ondra was a movie star she wasn't a star of a movie in which the people around here would go see.

The two leaned in close to talk until one made a comment the other didn't like then they would lean back as if backing out of the conversation then come back to make a new point. Danny asked her to meet him because he had a few offers that were brought to him for T's career. He never made a commitment on her behalf unless it was a guaranteed success. He was the one that told her to take the role that launched her fame. Also, the small roles in the straight to DVD films. They weren't great movies, but they did very well in sales which did very well for her bank account. The film that was about to be released, her first serious role was something she found and pushed for. Now he sat in front of her with 3 money opportunities. Two were not the best choices, but would keep her face and name out there. The other could lead to better things down the road.

"Danny are you fucking serious? I will not. Let me repeat that. I will not lower myself and be part of some fake bullshit reality show. Hell! I don't even know those chicks, so who is really going to believe we are friends?"

"That's where your acting comes in to play. Act like you all have been friends for a while."

"Next!"

"Well this one is......well this one is what it is."

Danny slid another folder across the table he took out of a briefcase that was sitting next to him on the floor. T'ondra moved the folder closer to her and opened it. Inside was a magazine and print out of a dollar amount and a few paragraphs. T' looked at the amount then at the magazine. "Hell, to the double no. I'm not getting naked for no mother fucking magazine. I don't give a damn how much they're offering."

"T'ondra...it's not that bad. Plus, you have shown most of your goodies on film anyway."

"So, what I've shown my titties and my ass in movies. I have never been completely butt ass naked in nothing. I either show the girls with bottoms on or my beautiful ass in a situation where I'm leaving out of a room or half covered in a bed. Did you read that shit they want me to do?"

"Yes, I did. The poses aren't bad on paper. Sitting in a chair with the girls up and out…"

T' then cuts him off, "Bent over that same chair with my ass up in the air and my pussy showing. My legs gapped wide open pinching my nipples and the worst fucking one was the shots with some other bitch……that would be nude too with her titties all in my face or some shit."

"Wasn't you with a woman for a hot second before?"

"Yes, I was, but that was private personal shit. No one else's business. Fuck that shit!"

"Ok, ok that one I admit was at the bottom of my list of proposals, but this one right here is the one…for now till a great role comes along. This is a good move I promise."

She looked at the proposal and up at Danny and asked if he was sure this would be the best move for right now. He gave her paperwork for a TV role. She wouldn't be the female star or even the second lead woman in the show, but it was a recurring role that was a comic relief type character. With Doves' talent it could be a scene stealer role. She leaned back, took a sip of her drink, thought for a minute and told Danny it had possibilities.

"How long do I have to make a decision on this?"

"Not long, but you do have a few days to think on it. They are getting the cast together now. They haven't seen your new movie yet so we are good on that, but I don't think it would matter, but who knows. The good thing is they asked if you were available for a few weeks to tape a pilot episode."

"Ok cool. Give me a day or two to roll it around in my mind and I'll give you an answer honey."

Danny agreed to her wishes and they spoke just a little while longer, then hugged, and went their separate ways. On the way home she thought about calling Andrea, but she always calls her. This is one of the times she wished she had a man in her life so she could get some help making decisions.

Back at home now, for a couple of hours, T'ondra sat in her kitchen with a full bottle of wine and an empty glass in front of her. She tapped her nails on the counter like someone with a nervous condition trying to roll around the good and bad of the offer Danny presented her. Usually when she had no one to talk to when things got difficult, she would find her solutions in a bottle of liquor or wine. This time though she tried really hard not to go down that path. It all was becoming very stressful and that wine was starting to call her when Scott came in the room and told her some of the material needed wasn't there, so he was ending the work day and her home was all hers again, but before he left out, he cocked his head sideways and stared at her.

"Ms. Dove is everything ok? You seem bothered."

"Oh, I'm fine...I guess. Just some career issues and choices to make that's all, but thank you for asking."

"Are you sure? I am quite the listener. I may not have the answer you need, but I promise to give any answer I come up with."

With a sigh T'ondra said, "OK you asked for it," and showed Scott the proposals her manager brought to her. He agreed the nude photo shoot would be a really bad career move. True she has shown the goodies in several movies, but it was for a character she was portraying. In a magazine she would be just another naked silent body with a staple in her belly. The reality show idea could lead to her being seen as a joke also. Even though most of that foolishness is scripted it still could hurt future projects.

Looking at the last folder the look on his face said he was taking a serious interest in this one. "Ms. Dove I believe this could be promising. There has been a lot of actors and actresses that have gone from movies to TV then back to movies with bigger roles and bigger checks. Plus, if the show is a hit it could last for a while and the rerun pay wouldn't hurt either."

"That's good shit there. I didn't look at that angle." They continued to talk and she realized she wasn't looking at him as a home contractor, but a man with intelligence. With good looks and a fine fuckin' body. She sat down her glass and walked passed him hitting him in the shoulder. "You know… you are alright there Mr. Mozell. Thank you for the honest advice."

"My pleasure. Besides I would've been broke if you chose to do that mag."

"Why is that?" She asked turning around behind him.

He turned to face her and says "Because I would've had to buy every copy I could find. That is being a super fan and all." Then he laughed.

Dove laughed too and walked back to him and kissed him on the cheek and says, "That's for being a super fan." Before she left out of the kitchen, she called his name. "Mr. Mozell…" He stands and turns to see her raise her shirt and let her lovely titties out. His mouth flew open and she ran out laughing.

A few days pass and the home improvements have been completed. Two small rooms were combined to create a large room with a vaulted ceiling accompanied by a huge window in the place of the small standard one that was there. In the kitchen the small island that sat in the middle was replaced with blue marble island sitting on a white ivory tile floor. As everything was being finished up Mozell and Dove played around like two teenagers with jokes being played on each other and eating lunches together. The two actually had become friends. The crew didn't mind the playing around either because Mozell had always been a laid-back boss as long as the work was done right and professionally. So, when they fooled around occasionally, he would just smile and shake his head. When the eyes of the workers weren't on them some of the playing involved smacks on the ass given by both.

Dove was overly satisfied with the work and Andrea said with all the improvements the value of her home almost doubled. Since the house was done she wanted the pool done next, but she took the offer for the TV show and it was about to start filming, so it had to wait because the show was being filmed on location out of town. The script was bought by a major studio and they had a request. That Dove's role be expanded to every episode one. They figured she had a loyal following and they would watch the show for her at first, even though she would never be naked on it. The day she was to leave she met with Mozell at her home to say thank you again and talk about future projects.

"Mr. Mozell…"

"Ms. Dove…considering we are now friends and I have palmed your ass. Which by the way is very soft and I have been flashed by you on a couple occasions, and on accident you have seen my manhood. So, I believe you can call me Scott."

"Ok Scott and by the way thank you for the soft ass compliment I worked hard for it and I really think the dick flash was a payback for the bikinis, but we'll go with the accident claim. Scott you are a great businessman and a good man as a friend. I would very much like to continue our business together when I get back."

"Why of course. I will keep my schedule flexible for you."

"Great I want you...I need for you to be here when I come back...for the project I mean."

She looked into his eyes and came up to him and hugged him. The embrace was more than a casual hug, more than friends hugging. There was some passion in it, some longing for more in it. Some I want you to be more in it.

She got in her car and drove away as Scott walked to his car. As he sat there another car pulled up five minutes later. Andrea Koss. He got out when she did.

"She finally gone Mr. Mozell?"

"Yes, she pulled off a few minutes ago."

She walks up to him and tells him let's get to it and she walks along the side of

T'ondras' home with a swing in her ass and keys in her hand.

"We gonna get caught doing this aren't we?"

"No Mr. Mozell. Not as long as you can get in and work quickly. How fast can you work your magic?"

"I usually don't do it for speed. I want to satisfy so quickness isn't something I normally do, but for you I will give it 100% at light speed."

"Good. Let's get to it then."

Chapter 6
What I Need vs What I Want

It has been a few days of filming and T'ondra was unexpectedly happy with being a cast member of this TV show. The other actors and actresses were cool as hell. Some were former movie stars like herself, but just a little bit older. Unlike the movie projects she had been on before, this group had no egos. No one thought they were better than the other, which made it a whole lot easier to come on set. If they messed a line up no one was yelling and screaming at them. They just kept right on going till someone couldn't take it anymore and fell out laughing.

It was day nine of shooting for the first seven episodes of the show. Originally, three were agreed on, but Dove's name being added gave the network reason to add four more. T'ondra sat in her trailer nervously. Today's episode recording had a more serious vibe to it. Her character was going to have a personal issue come up that mirrored her own life very closely. She was extremely nervous about the taping, do to the poorly reviewed film that was about to come out. Normally her nerves would've been settled with one or two or five drinks, but she decided to call her new friend Scott to lean on. After several attempts and no answer, she tried Andrea......no answer there either. "What the fuck? Where the hell is everyone!" She said a little too loudly than she would've liked, then her phone rang. With hopes that it was Scott returning her call she let a smile come across her face, but it soon disappeared when the pic and name came on screen…Danny Meek.

"Hello Danny, what is it? I'm about to go tape my scene, what's up?"

"Sweetie I want to give you some ok news and some good news!"

"Ok....that's a new phrase, never heard that one before. Give me the ok news first."

"Well....you won't have to worry about your show being hurt by bad reviews from that last movie."

"Ok news? That sounds like great news, but I thought the critics hated it?"

"That's where the good news comes in. It was so badly reviewed that the company decided to can the movie forever. No one outside the first group to see it will even know it exists. No promotion, no previews no nothing."

"So, if it's canned and I already got paid do I have to give my check back Danny? If so that remodeling I just did will erase a big chunk of my savings."

"The studio will just chalk it up as a loss. Wouldn't be the first time nor will it be the last. So, the cost of production, equipment, man-hour and crew pay will be included in that final loss total. Now someone may not get green-lighted for another film in quite a while, but that isn't on us. So, your money is your money."

Forgetting about the stress she just felt T'ondra felt like a huge weight was lifted off her shoulders. After hanging up with her manager she went out and nailed her seen like a pure professionally trained dramatic actress. Would never know she started off as a model.

This was the last day of filming for the show and everyone had a positive feeling that the network would pick the show up for an entire season. There was going to be a small after party for the crew, but Dove decided to make her trip home early. She never did get to talk to Scott or Andrea, but they did return her calls and left messages. Basically, playing phone tag. That's another reason she wanted to get back home as soon as possible to tell them how the taping went and the movie coming out being canceled. After her plane landed and she picked up her car from the parking garage T'ondra drove home still attempting to call her friends...no answers.

With a smile on her face T'ondra was very excited to get back in her remodeled home. When she came around the corner, she saw Scott Mozell's car sitting by the curb. That's odd she thought, he was finished with everything. Then as she pulled in her driveway she saw Andrea's car. In her mind the thought of what the fuck is this went through her mind. Getting out of the car she looked around and slowly went up the walkway until she heard voices coming from the back of the house.

"I can't believe we did it." A woman's voice said.

"I know I had to put in some hard work till I was finally satisfied." A man's voice answered.

Listening closely T'ondra recognized the voices as being Andrea and Scott. "I know these two haven't been using my house to meet up and fuck. She has a dude and knows I want to fuck Scott. Moving closer she continued to listen.

"Hell, I was satisfied with what you already did. That extra stuff was on you, but a wonderful touch. Too bad I can't get a little wet now, but we need to straighten things up before she gets here tomorrow." Andrea says.

"That's true it did get a little messy and I know what you're saying, I wouldn't mind getting wet myself."

"Both you motherfuckers can go get wet together in someone else's house dammit. How dare you two do this at my house of all places and Drea I thought you were my girl and I come home and find you've been on Scott's dick when you knew I wanted it."

Turning around in shock and mouths wide open Scott and Andrea looked at T'ondra then at each other then back at T'ondra. "What the hell are you talking about heffa? No one here has been doing anything! " Andrea yelled at T'ondra.

"That's right T'. We are here because we have a surprise for you." Scott tells her trying to break the tension with a smile.

"That's Ms. Dove to your punk ass bitch. How could you fuck my best friend in my house?"

The smile no longer was on Scott's face. "Well Ms. Dove... I don't know where you came up with that idea, but we were not here to have sex."

"I heard you two talking about getting wet and satisfied and putting in some hard work! That sounds like you were fucking the shit out of my friend!"

Taking a step away from T'ondra's direct eyesight he tells her, "Well you got part of that right, but it wasn't sex! Your friend wanted to surprise you by having your pool done before you got home. We got wet because we needed to know if the thing I've done to it was comfortable and done right. So, we got in part of it... with our clothes on!"

Andrea walked up into her face and spoke strongly, but softly to where only T' could hear her. "Listen here, you ungrateful bitch! You know me and I thought you knew I was your friend to the end. If you blast off like that at me again it will be the end, the end of this friendship!" Then Andrea shoulder bumped her knocking her back a step and went past her.

Now finally looking at her new pool, embarrassment was all over her face. She could hear Andrea's car start up and peel out as she raced away. Scott walked over to T'ondra now and tells her, "Don't worry about paying for this. It's already paid for and it wasn't pussy payments. We both went in together on this so enjoy it. Ms. Dove."

Reaching out she grabs his arm before he walks away and apologizes to him, telling him how sorry she was. Neither one of them answered her calls right away and she came home early and found their cars there together. With what she heard her mind went wild. She said she was so sorry, and could he please forgive her. She had so much going on that she wanted to tell them right when it happened.

"Well I guess I could see where your mind would lead you to believe something might have been going on, but that is your girl, plus she has a man. I don't get down like that. Involved women are a problem I don't need." Taking her hand and leading her to the edge of the pool he points out all the improvements to it.

The pool was already nice compared to others in the neighborhood, but Mozell took it to another level. It looked like the whole pool had been extended, but in fact he dug the shallow end up and walled it off making a hot tub. Also, the edge of the pool had been changed to a clear fiberglass top with lit cables in it so multiple arrays of colors would turn the water different colors. Also, they could be programmed to pulse with the beat of music. On the side a small area was made about the same size as the new hot tub and now was a new sitting area in the pool. It was only about 3 feet deep with a small bench made into the siding all the way around it with a floating table cabled to the bottom. The bench sat below the water level which was good because this area had a hard-top cover for when she and her friends just wanted to swim. So, this area could be closed off.

Looking at the pool she was absolutely thrilled. She turned and hugged him and said thank you repeatedly. T'ondra turned from him and started removing her clothes till she was completely nude then she jumped in the pool splashing water up on Scott. Frozen in place possibly from the cold water on his previous dry body or it could be seeing Doves nude body bouncing and swinging before it disappeared under the water. Coming up she smiled and motioned for him to join her. He smiled back and waved his hand saying no.

"You sure you don't want to join me? This is a very nice pool and I am all alone in it."

"Ms. Dove you have to be the Wildest client I have ever worked for. Since I am wet already a swim would seem like a great idea, but...I really must go so thanks, but no thanks." Scott told her with the biggest smile.

T'ondra swam back against the side of the pool and let her legs float up and open. With slight hesitation Scott removed his shirt and let it fall to the ground. She gave him the come here motion with her finger and told him no swimming allowed in her pool with pants on so he dropped his pants, walked to the edge and put his hands on his hips and asked if underwear was acceptable?

Looking at the well-shaped body of Mr. Mozell and the print that was bulging behind his compression shorts she smiled and said I guess so. He jumped in far enough from her making sure not to splash her…too much. Jumping in also made sure his entire body got wet at once keeping him from getting the chills. Scott came up right in between her legs. T'ondra was watching him underwater cruising like a fish, but didn't really expect him to surface so close, especially between her legs. He came up and the water ran down his chest and abs like water down a rock wall. Seeing his wet body so close turned her on and made her caramel nipples hard. She tried to wrap her legs around his waist, but he grabbed her ankles and held them apart. T'ondra pulled herself out of the pool and sat on the edge with legs still wide apart. Scott drank in the form of her body like a thirsty man drinking a refreshing beverage. His eyes scanned every inch of her, from the wet hair hanging on her shoulders, the soft brown of her eyes, the droplets of water falling off hard nipples to the low-cut handful of curly hair between thick thighs.

"T' I really appreciate the invite of the swim and the wonderful view before me, but I really must go. I need to meet my partner about a new business deal."

Saddened by his comment, but understanding of business before pleasure she told him no problem… anytime. They both got out of the pool and went inside both holding their clothes in hand. They had to hurry because there were no towels outside and didn't want to trail to much water inside on the floor.

After she dried off T'ondra stood in front of a large window in her bedroom that overlooked the patio and pool. She parted the drapes enough to get a good look at her yard and saw her neighbor and his wife in their yard sitting in patio chairs having drinks. The towel she dried off with was coming undone and fell to the floor just as Scott came around the corner with no shirt on and zipping up his pants with no underwear on because he had just swam in them. She knew he had come in, but didn't make any kind of move to cover herself up.

That skin color, those large breasts that sat up and could still be seen from behind, that perfect firm ass and....and....and how that brown peach hung down while her legs were slightly separated. Scott unzipped his pants and reached in his back pocket and took out his wallet to get a condom to put on, then let everything fall to the floor. As he moved closer to her, his cock became harder the closer he got. Using his foot against hers he opened her legs wider then cuffed her breast in his hands. As he kissed her neck, she threw the drapes completely open and put her hands against the glass. With a mind of its own his long very hard thick dark muscle of lust sank into her juicy chocolate peach. With slow deliberate thrusts he forced her vagina to accept every inch of him. Her eyes closed, and short moans came across her lips. As he pushed his pelvis hard against her ass he began to lift T'ondra off the floor to where she was only on her toes.

"Yes...give it to me, make me call your name. Make me explode on your dick. This pussy has been hungry for dick for so long, feed it, feed my starving kitten. Make it purr."

Scott let go of her breast then held her by the waist, pushing even harder now it made her lay against the large window. With the sounds of moans and groans mixing together Scott kept his eyes on T'ondras ass causing his cock to almost burst the condom he was wearing. Then he heard something like a low splashing. As he feeds her pussy more the sounds got louder and louder till a warm wet stream ran down his leg, but her legs were soaked from that peach juicing all over them. He had never felt a woman get so wet, well one woman almost drowned him because his tongue skills could be called unmatched, but this was unreal. He pulled almost all the way out and saw a puddle of cream in the curve of his erection. Cream was a strong turn on for him so he started pounding faster and actually raised her completely off the ground causing her to call his name… quite loudly. The wetness went from streams to a pool of her cum. Scott tells her he is coming so she quickly jumps off his dick and snatched off his condom, falling to her knees. Stroking his cock, he erupted all over her face and chest.

T'ondra laid back against the wall and Scott stumbled to it as well. They looked at each other exhausted and smiled then heard applause. Looking out the window they saw the neighbors looking up at them clapping. The neighbors got a special treat and saw the sex episode against the window. They raised their glasses to say cheers to the sex duo.

"What do you say, want another shower or is that appointment you had that important?" T'ondra asked with a smirk on her face.

Glancing out the window, then to T' then back outside. "I do believe I have a few moments more to spare, but without the extra eyes."

Chapter 7

Neglecting Responsibilities

It's been several weeks now since the encounter in the window and Scott has been spending most of his free time with T'ondra and some time that wasn't really free. He hadn't really been on the job sites like he should be. Although his crews are very trustworthy and capable of doing any job that comes their way, but having him on hand gave them a desire to do the very best work possible. With him gone they were doing acceptable work. He would be on site for consultations, and follow-ups, but his partner had to come in and check on and answer questions for the crew, Scott's normal job. Daryl Fenn was mainly the paper guy, the man in the office finding new clients and trying to expand the company not the hands-on construction guy. Instead of doing what was needed, Scott was meeting up with Ms. Dove in all kinds of places for sexual encounters. Parks early in the morning, her pool, bike trails, back of his truck bed, and once on the hood of her car in a parking garage, but the most outrageous place was in a restaurant waiting to be seated.

He sat in a corner on a bench with her on his lap. Since she wasn't the diva type, going to a nice restaurant like Miko' Italian Cuisine wasn't an issue. Miko's wasn't a $100 a plate type restaurant, but it was a casual business place. While waiting to be seated T'ondra sat on Scott's lap to give other people some room. Nothing too unusual about that except she was wearing a short skirt. Being a bit of an exhibitionist, she had unzipped his pants and stroked him behind her back till he was erect. Acting like she was readjusting herself on him she was actually sliding him inside of her. Unable to bounce up and down like she wanted to which would have definitely gotten them kicked out, T'ondra rocked back and forth with her legs crossed.

Swinging the top leg was actually a great cover for what she was doing. To any onlooker it seemed like she was being impatient or possibly holding her pee.

Whispering in her ear, "You are going to make me cum and you know I'm not wearing a condom."

She looked back over her shoulder and smiled, then his name was called for an open table. Scott's eyes became wide because he knew he had to get up with a hard cock hanging out of his pants. How in the hell was he going to hide himself?

Getting up T'ondra sat her purse in his lap blocking his dick from everyone's view. "Would you be a dear and hold this for me so I can straighten my skirt?"

She was good. He quickly stuffed himself back inside while she stood in front of him twisting and pulling on her skirt. Scott finally got up and handed her the purse. While eating Scott only thought of leaving so they could finish what she started. Before they finished eating she slid her hand in his lap, unzipped his pants again, pulled his thick muscle out and stoked him under the table till he exploded all over the bottom of the table. There was a long cloth covering the table, so no one had a clue.

After a couple weeks of no shows on job sites when he was really needed and postponed meetings with potential clients Daryl was fed up, he called Scott and demanded he meet him. Reluctantly Scott agreed, so they met the next evening at a sports bar.

"Scott you're my boy and I love ya like a brother, but you have been fucking up lately. Don't get me wrong, I'm beyond happy for you. Hell, you're knocking off a real-life movie star. Shit! I've jerked off to her in movies multiple times…"

"Whoa, whoa, whoa! That is way too much information to be sharing and I don't need or want to know that man!"

"My bad, but you know what I mean. Real talk, you need to get your shit together man." Then Daryl takes a sip of a beer.

The men ate a few wings they ordered and downed a couple more beers. Daryl broke it down to Scott on how his crew has been needing his expertise on site and his charm with getting new clients. He told him even though there is money in their bank accounts now it won't last forever. Scott agreed and said he was sorry for neglecting his job. Promising to get his shit together they raised their beer mugs and tap them together.

"You can have your sex time with your fantasy woman, but make sure you bring your ass to work man!"

"I got you bro, the sex is good, damn good. Honestly, it's that hot shit, but I need that money man."

The two continued to eat, drink, and yell at the screens showing various games. Daryl told Scott about running into an old friend from college, but not who, and that they needed to set up an outing so everyone could get caught back up. Scott told him about how well T'ondra's television show was going and she was positive about the possibility of it getting picked up for another season. Daryl told him to congratulate her for him. He didn't get to see her that often because she was either on set taping or they were out together at some secluded spot on the low, but she did know who he was.

After eating too much and drinking way too much they called it a night by contacting an Uber and leaving their vehicles there. Not being as drunk as Daryl, Scott remembered to tell management what was up with the two cars that would still be there after closing and they would be back to get them tomorrow. They bro-hugged and told each other later and went separate ways.

Chapter 8

Life of A Star

It has been a while since Daryl had to straighten Scott out about his lack of leadership with the crew. Back on track Scott has been spending more time on sites and being more available to his crew. Still not taking on as many new projects as Daryl would have liked, but the quality of workmanship was once again at its best. Everyone was happy except for T'ondra, with Scott spending more time on the work sites that cut out attention time for her. During those absent times she was filling glasses with alcohol. She would wonder if Scott was spending time with other female clients like he did with her.

Even though things weren't going the way she wanted with Scott, the TV show was going extremely well. So well that all the actors on the show were now getting invited to red carpet events. By T'ondra being a former movie star, the invites were a welcomed reminder of her former glory, but she was a no-show to every event. Then an invitation came that caught her attention. It wasn't an average carpet walk like the others, this was A-listers. The hottest movie stars around, not just who is hot now and for them to invite her could mean a return to the big screen. She called Scott to tell him all about it, but before she could finish dialing his number, he called her.

"Well hello there Mr. Mozell, I was just about to call you."

"Oh really? What's on your mind sweet tea?" Scott had begun to give T'ondra little nicknames which are common in relationships, but she never gave any to him. Secretly this bothered Scott. Why wouldn't she play along with the cute name game? She gave him names though, but it was only while having sex. He even tried singing to her at times, but she usually laughed at him or told him how bad he sounded.

"Scott! I got something to tell you! I got an invitation to walk the red carpet at The Screen Legends Award ceremony."

"Never heard of that award."

"Well it's not a show exactly. They give out awards to legendary actors and actresses who are still making films, but not the big budget movies. Most of them aren't considered television worthy any more so no network will air it, but everyone nominated really appreciates being honored still. Trust me it's still a huge deal to be invited to attend. Only the most popular, talented and up and coming people will be there."

"Well that sounds great, when is it?"

"Next week. The only problem is that I don't have anyone to walk the carpet with. I can't take Andrea because they will think I'm WITH her! Can't go with Danny my manager either, bad look. Should I decline?"

Scott sat silently, but in his mind, there were all kinds of things being said. What the hell? Is he not good enough? Does she think he is not stylish enough to walk the carpet, let alone accompany her to the event? He wanted to curse her out, but that's something he promised himself he wouldn't do. After seeing his mom being verbally abused by his father, and sister being abused and killed by her boyfriend, he would only treat a woman like a goddess... that's if she deserved it. Otherwise she would get common respect.

"Uhhh T'...if you need a date, I would be more than happy to go with you... If I'm good enough to make your body vibrate after sex, I think I'm good enough to...well I wouldn't embarrass you or make an ass of myself."

Dove held her phone silently. She never even considered asking Mozell to accompany her to the awards, but before she answered T'ondra pictured Scotts body. First naked which wasn't really helpful right now because it started to make her cat purr, then his body in a nice fitted tuxedo. He is very pleasant to look at. Plus, by not being an industry man there wouldn't be much desire for him by other women.

Most…well…practically all women in movie town want a man that is somebody and could possibly upgrade their career, not a man to be an anchor in her life.

"You know what Scott....I would be most delighted if you would go with me. Can you free up some time for next week? The show is on a Tuesday evening."

"Tuesday evening? Why would they have it on a Tuesday and not the weekend?" Scott asked puzzled.

"Well there is usually something happening on the weekends there and a lot of them have… ahh…parties on the weekends. So, catching them early in the week is best for participation."

"I understand now. Glad you're not in that lifestyle."

T'ondra agreed that she was also glad, but in her mind, she knew that at one time she was indeed in that life. Drugs weren't her vice, but alcohol on the other hand is another story and quiet as kept it is still a monkey on her back. At times after excessive drinking she would wake up nude in places she never remembered going to. Luckily, she had good people around her that kept her from being taken advantage of. She had been caught giving oral sex to a few cast members, and they were married, who could they tell. The worst was when Andrea saved her before a nasty ass director filmed her having real sex in a scene for his movie. He told the actor with her to give her a few drinks to loosen her up before the scene. He knew about her drinking issues, so he planned to film the sex and then cut it out of the movie, but the cut would be saved for his personal use.

Dove was very comfortable being seminude on camera, but when Andrea happened to be on set that day and smelled the liquor on T' before the shoot, and saw the actor massaging his cock to get it hard she knew this was not part of the scene so she interrupted and pulled Dove away to her trailer to sober up. Once sober T'ondra came back and cursed the director out and kicked the actor in the balls. Needless to say, she was replaced. Sadly, the actress that took her place had a pill habit and was filmed having real sex, the cut footage was leaked, and her career destroyed.

"Well Mr. Mozell plane tickets will be on me if you can cover hotel cost?"

"Ms. Dove that sounds fair. So, when do I leave?"

"Sunday morning. Maybe we could spend a day with my cast members since we are in mid-season holding."

"Whatever the lady would like."

Scott made sure to run everything past his partner to avoid any problems. There was nothing that would need his direct involvement for a couple days, he was free to enjoy himself. The flight was great, Scott had never been cross country and meeting the actors of a hit TV show was amazing. Then came the night of the event. T'ondra was stunning wearing a burgundy dress that had thin straps on the shoulder and dipped slightly with clear fabric over the cleavage giving the appearance that her large breast could spill out at any moment but was completely supported. With faint gold accents throughout the dress, dazzled when hit by lights. To top it off a semi-long train kissed the ground off her left leg. Scott wore a traditional black tux with a very close in color burgundy shirt with a black cuff and collar.

As T'ondra stepped out of the limo provided by event staff the photos went off like strobe lights., but when Scott came out, they paused, and murmurs began.

"That's Dove, but who the hell is that guy?"

Stepping on the carpet the flashes were still not popping until another guy stepped onto the walkway... Jordan Juss. The hottest actor in town and has been for a couple years now. Even his suck ass movies pull in mega millions just because he has the lead role. Also, secretly he is Ms. Dove's celebrity crush.

Dove walked slightly in front of Mozell, but both of them stopped when they saw Juss. He walked up and gave Scott a pat on the back and said what up guy, then he took a step closer to T'ondra and smiled. Just like a school girl at a boy band concert she felt her knees begin to buckle. Jordan Juss was in front of her and smiling at her.

Somewhere behind all the flashing lights a photographer said, "Hey, why don't you two stands together for a picture. You! Guy no one knows, could you move back and out of the shot please?"

Embarrassed and feeling very out of place now he said nothing and backed away. Seeing T'ondra posing for the pictures put a small smile on his face until that Jordan guy put his arm around her back which may not seem like a big deal since it was for the paparazzi, but from Scott's viewpoint he could see the son of a bitch clearly had his hand on her ass. Not just on her ass, he was palming the damn thing. His tiny smile quickly turns into a look of aggression.

Seeing the look on Scott's face T'ondra motioned with her hand that was behind Juss ' back to calm down and it was ok. At that moment a show coordinator came out and saw the two actors together and clapped his hands together saying, "This is perfect. The hottest male movie actor coming down the red carpet with possibly the hottest female television actress right now. Right this way please hurry because we're about to begin and don't worry we have seats right up front."

Scott watches the two being shuffled inside and leaving him alone outside. A journalist that was watching the whole thing came up to Scott and said, "Tough break my man, but that's the nature of the town. It won't be with everyone else sitting, but I can get you in with me and perhaps you can catch up with her at the first break."

Scott told him thank you and he appreciated his help and that drinks would be on him that night back at wherever they were headed. The guy said that sounded like a plan, then they shook hands and headed for a side entrance where the press was going through.

"Oh...by the way my name is Gerry, Gerry Grace and you and Ms. Dove made a fine-looking couple."

Scott responded by telling Gerry his name and saying thank you, but right now he wasn't sure of how much of a couple they were.

Chapter 9
Fed Up

After the embarrassment at the awards on the red carpet Mozell and Dove had a long talk on the way home. Scott told her how he felt being left outside while she was ushered inside with another man. A famous man, but another man none the less. She laughed it off and told him it happens all the time, the coordinators often pair celebrities together because they give good face or it's a publicity stunt to get people talking about them to upgrade their popularity. Scott thought about it for a while and it made sense… kind of.

As he sat back in the corner of the limo letting it all sink in T'ondra reached over and unzipped his pants. Before he could even put up a fight his penis was out, hard, and in her mouth. There was no partition keeping the driver from seeing what she was doing, but Dove didn't care, she was doing what she thought would make it all better between them. Instead of continuing to have a nice conversation she went straight to a sexual act. Eyes closed and suction so strong his butt was off the seat, Scott just let her have her way with him. With the way she was tasting him it didn't take long for him to climax. She licked her lips to clean off any excess man cream and took out her cell phone to upload some new selfies. Scott put himself back in his pants and stared out the window for the rest of the ride to the hotel.

Back home in the city now for about a month ...the relationship...between Mozell and Dove hadn't gotten any better, nor had it gotten any worse. They still would meet up for vigorous sex sessions and constantly talk on the phone. She was back and forth in and out of town filming the television show and he was chin deep in his remodeling business. Then one day while driving home from another weekend of filming T'ondra got a phone call from Danny Meek.

"T' are you sitting down?"

"Oh shit! The show just got canceled didn't it? I knew things were going too good for me." After she asked the question all of a sudden, she had a taste for whiskey, her cure-all antidote.

"No girl. Stop going straight negative on me. A matter of fact I have good, borderline great news. Jordan Juss himself called me about... YOU...DOING... A...MOVIE... with him. How does that sound?"

"Danny! Don't fuck with me like that, you know I am the biggest Juss fan."

"Well the role isn't a big role. You'll be playing an ex-girlfriend role that his character happens to run back into, but hold on to your ass, you will have one of the two sex scenes in the movie with yours being the most intense..."

Before Danny could finish T'ondra shouted yes, yes, yes! She didn't care about how much she was being offered or how long she would be on screen. All she knew now was that she would be kissing her crush Jordan Juss!!!!

Danny finally got to finish telling her about the details and when she should expect a copy of the contract. After they hung up she immediately called Scott to tell him the good news… well good news to her, Scott was no longer a fan of Jordan Juss. T'ondra reassured him that he was just a fellow actor and this role could possibly catapult her back onto the big screen. Not only back, but in something other than a comedic appearance. He agreed with that and wanted to support her any way he could.

About a week had passed since Dove got the call from her agent and she now knew all that she needed to know about the movie. The filming of her part should only take one day if they start early in the morning. She asked Mozell if he would accompany her to the filming and be on set while they filmed. This excited Scott, being on an actual movie sound stage and seeing it being filmed! There was no need to tell his partner about going out of town this time because he would only be gone a day. A flight was booked and by weeks end they were in the air and on their way.

Once there at the studio T'ondra Dove was greeted and shown where her dressing room was. Scott Mozell was given a backstage pass and a tour of the soundstage while Ms. Dove got ready.

T'ondra sat in a chair waiting impatiently just having her make-up finished when Jordan walked in with two glasses in his hands. Her eyes got wide and her mouth parted to speak, but nothing came out. On the other hand, her kitten between her legs began to purr and twitch. Her panties would be getting wet if she was dressed yet, but she didn't want to get make-up on her clothes for the movie, so she was still in a robe. He heard she was nervous about the scene they would be filming first... the sex scene. They wanted it done and out of the way early.

"Ms. Dove I am a huge fan of yours. This is truly an honor for me to be working with you."

"Thank you, but the honor is mine. You are the number one box office draw in town for the last few years and here I am about to shoot a scene with you."

They conversated a little while longer as he tried to put her at ease by offering her the glass he brought in. She drank and talked and talked and drank. Knowing her issues with alcohol she drank anyway. Shit, Jordan Juss gave it to her; how could she not accept it and drink it. Quickly she felt warm and woozy and for some reason horny. Then a call came through an intercom in the dressing room.

Dove, 30 minutes till filming. Dove, 30 minutes till filming please report to the soundstage. She quickly got up and stumbled but balanced herself. Juss was already dressed and said to go ahead and get dressed. I'll see you out there, let's make some magic. On his way out, he saw her underclothes on a roller cart next to her movie outfit. Passing by he took the panties and slipped them in his pocket while her back was turned. He smirked and patted his pocket as he went out of the room.

T'ondra walked out to the soundstage feeling a little woozy like she just had about 6 shots of liquor at once. She hid her condition very well because being tipsy or drunk for that matter, is something she was used to while filming. For a moment or two she was concerned about her outfit for the scene. The white blazer top with a red shirt that was underneath that made her breast sit up so well was very sexy to her. The wide stripped red and white skirt was making her legs look extra nice, but the skirt was very short. This still wasn't what was bothering her. The lack of panties was. True she has gone underwear-less in movies before, but she had some kind of pants on. Then the drink she had begun to mellow her out. She thought to herself, to hell with it.

Scott was led to a seat behind the camera and sound men who were next to the director. Seeing Dove act in person was such a thrill for Scott, not only has he done a job for her, he has been having sex with her. He felt they were more than friends now. Well in his mind they were anyway. Now he is on set watching her do what she does best. The way she moved, the way she looked as she spoke her lines; Scott was like a kid in utter amazement. After a very short, maybe three or four minute break, it was time for the sex scene.

He kissed her. So, what, just acting kissing. Then he removed her top and caressed her breasts. Her titties have been touched in movies before. Then he sucks on her nipples. Ok. He guessed, but why were they hard? It wasn't cold or chilly in there. When Jordan lifted T'ondra up and on the bed, Scott began to squirm in his seat a little. Not knowing about the panties was probably a good thing. First of all, he simply didn't know. Another reason was he couldn't see from his seat behind everyone, but the camera and sound guys could. Juss lifted her skirt to her waist and leaned her back. The two crew guys looked at each other wide-eyed and smiled then went back to the action. When Juss let his pants fall to his ankles and kicked them off is when Scott couldn't watch anymore. Seeing him having simulated sex with T'ondra was more than he could take so he got up quietly and went to the beverage table just around the corner.

After about 15 minutes he heard the director say cut, then the two crew members he was behind came out laughing and slapping five to each other. They knew the man was a fan of Dove's, but not that they were there together. They came over to him and asked if he saw that shit not knowing he had left. When he said he stepped out after Juss showed his bare ass, they filled him in on what he missed.

"Man! He fucked her! I mean he fucked her for real and raw dog!"

"What? All that was fake shit they do in the movies."

"No, no my man." The camera guy says overly excited. "She wasn't wearing underwear and he was naked for real like he usually does when he has to take off his pants. From our point of view, we saw he was hard and saw it go in her."

"Hell yeah! He fucked her till he busted, and he busted inside her. Could see it running out when he pulled out going soft."

Scott was speechless. Hurt and anger fought for control of his emotions. He wanted to confront her immediately, but his legs were stuck in place. Stuck listening to them talk about how his... whatever... just got fucked in front of him. After the two guys finished and left, he stormed out of the soundstage and headed straight for her trailer.

If steam could actually come from someone when they were mad, Scott would have sounded like a tea kettle. He didn't even bother to knock on the door. He grabbed the door and yanked it open. Before, he was having a battle within himself about being hurt or angry. It was no longer a fight, hurt won hands down. As the door opened he saw T'ondra bent over in a chair getting fucked from behind by Jordan. True they weren't officially together, but the pain was most definitely real. They locked eyes without a word first then T'ondra patted Jordan on his arm to get him to stop fucking her. The rush of the alcohol had worn off some time ago so this was free will. Jordan finally pulled himself out of her and used her top to wipe his penis off, then he moved to the back of the trailer. Dove grabbed a robe and met Scott at the door. She never apologized for what she was doing. Only for him seeing it. She told him this was Jordan Juss, a megastar, how could she pass it up? To Scott her voice trailed off to silence in his ears. Her mouth was moving, but no sound. She came closer and tried to hug him, but he jumped back and gave her a very angry look.

"Scott this doesn't mean anything. It's just a fuck. Now give me a few minutes while I say goodbye to Jordan and I'll be out to go to lunch with you." She turned and closed the door behind her.

A single tear fell from Scott's eye, then he turned and walked away without a word. He then went right to the hotel and got his things and called a cab to take him to the airport. He never even called her to say he was leaving. He just got on the plane and left any feelings he had for her there in the trailer. The fantasy of being with his crush just became a tragic nightmare. Fuck that life, he was better than being a celebrity's side dick or plaything.

Chapter 10

Is That Really You!?

A few weeks passed and Scott had become a wreck of a man. He still showed up at work, but he wasn't his normal cheerful self. Short tempered, but not mean to his workers. A no-nonsense approach to work is a better description of how it was now. Scott stopped playing around and joking with the crew, get the job done and go home. When he went home he tried to fix his hurt feelings by drowning them in bottles and bottles of liquor. Although he never came to work drunk, the after-effects were still there. He would sit at home and question what had happened. What did he do to her to make her treat him that way? Or not do? Did he do anything to her at all, or was this just the way she was?

One night before he could open another bottle, he got a call from Daryl asking him to come join him at Club Chocolate Silk. Chocolate Silk has been the hottest spot in town for a while now. The original owner was killed in an accident while taking a drunken female patron home. Some say he knew her, but he had never been seen with her out anywhere and was not the woman he was supposedly dating. The club was under new ownership now, but everything still ran the same. Must still be under the original management.

As usual, the club was pumping and it was packed. Scott looked around and saw Daryl upstairs in the window of one of the club's private rooms. He waived down to Scott and pointed towards the elevator up.

The elevator doors opened upstairs and Scott walked out. He was greeted by Daryl with a bro handshake and chest bump, but before he could say hello, he heard...

"Chubbs...Chubbs Mozell is that you?!"

Back in high school and his first two years of college Scott was a little heavy. He hated being called fat though. Except for one person. Better yet four people, three women and a cool ass guy that was a boyfriend to one of them. He knew none of them meant any ill will towards him by calling him Chubbs, so they got away with it. It has been a long, long time since he has heard that name and the voice it came from sounded real, real familiar. Looking over Daryl's shoulder he saw the source of the voice calling him.

"Ahh hell no! It can't be! Is that you Dom?"

"Chubbs Mozell!!! Come here and give me a hug. Damn Chubbs, you're not chubby anymore!"

"Sure isn't. Scott is looking really good."

While hugging one woman, another steps through the crowd and flashes a smile. "Robin Kyle. Is that you?"

"Robin Lock now, and it's me sugar."

"Lock? As in Gerald big brother Lock? You two finally got married? Congratulations." He came over and hugged Robin just as tight as he did Dom. They all called her Dom, but her name is Dominece. Then his ears had the fortune to hear a voice that was like a seductive song. Looking in the direction of the voice he finally saw her... her... the one he had a crush on since middle school. Then a thick, gorgeous woman came through the crowd like a queen through her subjects. Scott's mouth dropped open, but he closed it quickly because he wanted to make a good first impression since it's been many years since he saw her... her!!

"Hello Chubbs, you look great. Hope you haven't forgotten about me hun."

"I look average, you look great. I mean you haven't changed since college." Then he breaks into song. "The men all pause when you walk into the room, the men all pause." Daryl disappears while Scott walks into the middle of the ladies singing. About three or four minutes later Klymaxx plays through the sound system.... The Men All Pause...the three ladies take Scott's hands and lead him down to the dance floor and turns the floor out. As all four dance around, Daryl stands off to the side sipping a drink smiling, thinking this is just what he needed.

After working it out to at least 7 songs in a row they all return upstairs to the private V.I.P room. Sitting and wiping sweat off their faces, they ask for water from the private waiter that served that room. Everyone, but Dom, she ordered a double Henny and Coke, typical Dom. Scott downs his water rather quickly then turns his attention to the women. One in particular.

"Shanette Tolls, how have you been? I haven't seen you and The Crew since I had to leave school my sophomore year."

"I'm doing extremely well now. I had a really rough time sometime back, but my friends old and new held me down so I survived and I'm good. By the way I am so sorry to hear about your parents passing."

"Thank you. Dad went then mom said her life light was gone and I was able to take care of myself, so she went shortly after."

"That is so sad and beautiful at the same time Chubbs." Robin tells him as she touches his hand.

Scott nods his thank you then looks at the group and asks "I see The Crew is a member short tonight. Where is Anita Watts?"

Then the mood of the table changed. Robin had a frown on her face and Dom went on a cursing frenzy till Shanette told her to be quiet and finish her drink. Daryl said, "Hot damn! Ya'll just turned smooth evil. What did she do? I know her legs would fly open at the drop of an expensive hat just like Domineces' mouth would, but she never got ya'll this upset before!"

Shanette spoke up and said, "Let's just say she made a huge mistake that hasn't and may never be forgiven. The Crew is down to a trio now."

Daryl looked over at Dominece and raised an eyebrow.

"Damn right! She got knocked the fuck out. About four times or every time she tried to speak and apologize. I forget which and if she would show up here. Number five coming her way." Then she and Daryl slapped hands, laughed and clink glasses.

Mozell threw up his hands as to say he surrendered to this conversation. He asked Robin about Gerald and found out he was running not one, but several repair shops in a couple states and Robin had become a head nurse in the city's biggest hospital. Dominece was working at the auto factory and just got asked to be a supervisor, that's why they were in the club that night. Daryl happened to bump into Dominece at the gas station last month. When he found out about Shanette he was blown away. She had also worked at the factory and quit, then used her degree and became an executive working downtown in the business district. Sadly, to hear she lost a recent love to a senseless murder coming from an ex-guy friend of Anita's.

The night ended with Scott telling his friend and partner Daryl thank you for getting him out and showing him the world still revolved without T'ondra in his life, as well as reuniting him with The Crew, especially Shanette. They all promised to keep in touch now that they are back in touch. On the way home Scott got a text from all three ladies and even got a text from Gerald, saying how glad he was that The Crew bumped into him and that the guys have to get together and hang sometime soon. It was the text from Shanette that held his attention mostly. It said, "It was so good to see you again Chubbs lol...we need to have lunch soon to catch up for real. Besides we have questions from the past that needs to be answered. Call or text me to set it up Chubbs..."

A smile came across his face as he thought, I will call tomorrow afternoon. For the first time in a while T'ondra Dove was nowhere in his thoughts and he felt good.

Chapter 11

Open or Closed

The next weekend after wrapping up the final paperwork on a job for an up and coming hip-hop artist, Scott tells Daryl who was on site with him more often now, that he was heading home and could he make the tool and supply check. Daryl said sure, he had it covered. Besides he had time to waste because he had nothing planned to do that evening.

While in his truck Scott decided to give Shanette a "what's up" call or at least leave a message. To his surprise she answered.

"Hello...hey Chubbs, what's good with you?"

"Nothing much, just ending a long day at work. I was calling to see when you would like to get together for that talk."

"Well...you know what? I just ended a stressful day myself. How about dinner tonight if you're not too tired?"

"Miss a chance to have dinner with a lovely lady, I think not. I need to shower so how about in an hour at that new place called Rooftop Overview?"

"Oh, that new restaurant that's downtown overlooking the river? I've been wanting to go there since it opened, but had no one to go with. You know Dom would turn that place out if I took her."

"True that. She was always a wild card. Would you like me to pick you up? Would hate for you to waste time looking for a space or paying valet."

"How sweet. Sure, you can come get me Chubbs."

Shanette gave Scott her address and they both got ready for their dinner rendezvous. Scott called her to say he was on the way. Not to rush her, but to give her a heads up on how long it would take for him to get there. Pulling up on time Scott got out of his car and rang the doorbell. Stepping back a couple feet out of the doorway he waited with an arm behind his back. Shanette answered her door looking gorgeous with black skin-tight jeans and a simple navy-blue blouse. Her hair was pulled into a ponytail. Scott was awestruck. He handed her a single purple rose. Shanette once received a boutique of purple roses after a really bad breakup in college, she never knew who sent them because they were laid at her doorway. She just figured it was one of The Crew because not too many knew one of her favorite colors was purple then. Now her old friend stands in front of her with a purple rose.

"It was you! Back then. The bouquet in the doorway in college. After Elis got that freshman cheerleader pregnant, I was so hurt till I saw those flowers, it meant so much to me."

"You are oh so welcome, for then and now."

The two sat at dinner reminiscing on their college days before Scott had to drop out and catching him up on what went on afterward too. When the question from Shanette of what happened to their closeness came up Scott lost the smile on his face and dropped his head. He told her that he couldn't be more to her then than just a friend. With the fresh break up she was dealing with a romance with a real good male friend wouldn't be good for her. She needed her girls around her and a true friend's shoulder to lean on.

Anger began to rise in her till she thought about what he said. It was true, Scott would've been just a rebound relationship. She reached across the table and raised his head up. "Thank you for being such a good friend. Now that has been cleared up, let's let the past be the past."

By the time dessert came out Shanette was asking him about his love life. He took a bite of the slice of red velvet cake he ordered, then took a deep breath. "There was this chick I was with shortly before I started my business. It all began cool as hell, then it all took a turn down shit lane."

"Wow! That sounds bad, what went down Chubbs?"

"Her name was Lyanna and we were about to get engaged, well I was going to ask till I realized she couldn't keep her legs closed. I forgave her the first time because her lie was real damn good, but one night me and Daryl went out and she stayed home claiming to be sick. Unfortunately, we called it a night about an hour after being out, we just got a bottle and rode around till it was gone. I had Daryl drop me off at her spot. Since I had a key, I went right on in to take care of her because she was, well, sick. When I went back into her bedroom, I found her being fucked in the ass by a guy she introduced to me as her cousin."

"The old cousin games. Seen it done by Anita many times Chubbs. I'm so sorry."

"After seeing that shit, I took the bottle I had brought for us and walked home downing the bottle walking 15 blocks drinking the whole way. From then on liquor was my pain remedy. Well until me and Daryl went into business together."

He told her that he has brought the mood of the evening down long enough, so he asked her if she ever got married and how have the men in her life been treating her. Shanette told him there weren't many guys that came into her world that was worthy enough to stay for any period of time. Then she left the assembly factory and joined the downtown workforce. With hard work she became an executive associate at the Donovan Modeling Agency. Then she meets the man of her dreams, Anthony Regal. He owned Chocolate Silk and hired her company to get it off the ground. They had a great connection with each other that was cut short by one of Anita's ex-boyfriends that tried to end her, but killed him instead. The manager of the club told her as long as there was a club there, her and her group never had to spend a penny to get in, or for anything the place provided.

Scott slid around the table and hugged her. The comfort of his embrace was so warm and welcoming. A feeling she hadn't felt in a long time and one she missed and welcomed back.

They playfully argued on who would pay for dinner with Scott winning by taking her purse and dropping it in a chair next to him; which he put his leg on to keep her from getting it back. As they left, she suggested that he come by her office because they had been considering expanding. Now that she had a good friend that did that kind of work, she wanted him to get that business. He agreed to come by as soon as he finished up with his last client the next day.

Taking Shanette home, Scott walked her to the door and hugged her again. For a second their eyes locked and hearts paused. On any other date he would give his date a light kiss, but this was Shanette Tolls, his heart sang for her since senior year of high school. He moved closer to her and bit on her neck like a toothless vampire causing her to burst into laughter. He smiled, turned and got in his car and pulled away. In her doorway she was still laughing rubbing her neck. Something was very familiar about this, she thought.

Chapter 12

I Put My Name on It

It has now been close to two months since Scott walked in on T'ondra having sex with Jordan Juss. The movie they were filming was put on hold right before it was completed due to allegations of Juss having forced sex with most of the women on set, like make-up and costume women. Usually things like this are swept under the rugs with payoffs and firings, but one of the women that told was a young cousin to one of the major producers of the film. Since the film wasn't completed most of the actors didn't get paid and Dove was one of them. This movie has cost her way more than she wanted. First of all, she wasn't getting paid, secondly, they told her she would be in more scenes, so she had to take too much time away from the television show, which in part wrote her character off the show. Lastly, she lost her motivational dick, Scott. Jordan was a great quick fuck, but Scott was on call lasting pleasure and now even he was gone.

For the last couple days all T'ondra did was drink. Drink heavily and often. Andrea needed to come by quite frequently to make sure she wasn't passed out naked outside, again Andrea told her Scott was a good dude and good for her mentally not just physically, but all Dove got out of those conversations was that she needed a good fucking to get her life back on track. In between drinking binges, she told her friend that she has been trying to call Scott, but he doesn't answer or return her calls. Drea suggested that she go by his house, but T' said they usually meet up somewhere and she wasn't sure where he lived.

"What you mean you don't know where he lives? This man has been inside you, numerous times and please don't tell me, but probably in your mouth and ass too and he never took you to his place?"

112

"Well he always invited me over, but I thought it would be sexier to get it on in a park or family restroom at the mall."

"So, YOU just wanted HIM for sex?! Bitch do you have any idea how many black unicorns there are out here?"

"Black Unicorn? What the fuck that mean?"

"A black man with a good job, his own place, not one, but two vehicles, no police record, single with no kids; bitch, wake up. That is ultra-rare... black unicorn!"

"Damn! He was all that? I just thought of him as some thunder cock on call."

Andrea shook her head at her friend then took the half-empty bottle off the counter and poured it out. Turning to T'ondra she told her you're in luck my slut ass friend, although you don't know where he is, I do. I have a neighbor that works downtown that was telling me about this fine ass man that owns a remodeling business doing some work at the Donovan Agency.

"Donovan!" Then she laughed and said "I know exactly where that is."

"Oh, by the way, word also is he is seeing one of the women that work there."

"Guess he downgraded. Went from a star to a young model. I'll put that little bitch in her place and make him beg to be sipping on this pussy again. I will make my grand entrance down there bright and early Monday morning."

T'ondra Dove stepped out of her car in front of a black office building downtown Monday morning like the former headlining movie star she used to be. Wearing a dark red skirt that came to the middle of her thighs with a red lace top and a black jacket over the top. With a swing of her hair she walked inside and looked around. There were lots of people in suits walking around on cell phones. Moving past them like a queen would do peasants, a security guard got her attention and asked her could he help.

"Hey Ms. Fine what can I do to help YOU out sweet thang?"

Dove looked him up and down over the top of her glasses. With a twist of her lips she walked on without a word to him because she knew where she was going.

"Ms. Fine, if you find yourself needing some assistance come on back so Vic can do anything you want."

Entering the elevator Dove thinks to herself, *I still got it with these nothing ass dudes.* As she rides up in the elevator T'ondra remembers getting her start as a model here at the Donovan Agency. Such a nice little place to work as a youngster. Right before the door opened, she tries to remember which office the agency was in, then the elevator opens.

T'ondra stood outside the elevator with her jaw dropped. What used to be a quarter of that floor with about six separate offices on the floor was now the whole floor and was widened to just one office. Thinking this couldn't be Donovan's she looked around until she saw the reception desk. No…Reception area…with no Ms. Toni in sight, she must have gotten fired Dove thought. What she thought would be a small office like she remembered was in fact a whole floor as an office. Looking around at the beautiful young women sitting waiting to be interviewed she noticed a huge glass window on one side of the floor saying Jack Arms and on the opposite side was an equally large window with Toni Jerson. In utter amazement T'ondra just stood in the middle of the room looking, just then a very well-dressed woman came out of the elevator followed by Scott Mozell. Both of them were smiling and laughing.

"Oh my god! T'ondra Dove is in the office! I am such a huge fan of yours." The woman said as she reached out to shake the stars hand. Scott's face showed a very different expression.

"So, this is the little bitch taking up my time with you now Scott? You wanna ignore a star for one of her groupies?"

"Excuse me! Ms. Dove I am a fan, but I am not one of your groupies!"

"T'ondra! What the hell are you doing here? How did you know I would be here?"

"The better question is what are you doing here?"

"I remodeled the floor for the Donovan Agency. Why are YOU here?"

"Andrea told me you are fucking some new young bitch now."

"This is a place of business Ms. Dove. I will ask you nicely one time to please not use that type of language in my place of business."

"Your place of business?! Little tramp you are a wannabe model trying to be something. I am something!"

"T'ondra this is my friend Shanette, and besides we are no longer together. If in fact we ever were!"

Shanette felt the hood blood in her rising, but she took a deep breath and composed herself. "I am not a model, but thank you for the compliment. In fact, I am…"

Before she could finish T'ondra cut her off continuing to curse her out very loudly. Shanette didn't back down pushing Scott's hand away as he tried to pull her back and trying to calm Dove down enough to listen.

"Bitch, I don't care what you think you are. Just know this is the face that made this place to begin with."

Just then an older voice came from the back silencing everyone. "Excuse me? Who made this place? True you were one of the first models here, but rest assured you had nothing and I repeat nothing to do with making this agency!"

Then a man's voice followed. A voice that had a slight accent, but commanded attention. "That's right! And as I remember she was very difficult to work with then. I see nothing has changed with her attitude since going to Hollywood."

The three turned to see Mrs. Donovan and Jack Arms walking towards them. The CEO and Co-Vice President. T'ondra Dove became silent as her former employers stepped to her with extreme authority.

Shanette bumped T'ondra as she walked past her. "Mrs. Donovan, I apologize for this outburst in here."

"No need to apologize dear. We heard everything from Toni's office while we were getting it ready for her after her vacation. "

"Vikki I am sorry to curse out your little model chick here, but she is with my dick right there. "

That's Mrs. Donovan to you T'ondra! Also Ms. Tolls here is not one of our models. She is our Chief Executive in charge of business relations! And it doesn't matter who this man belongs to. He is someone hired to do a job for us so technically he is our employee too. With her title Ms. Shanette Tolls is something. An executive! So please give her the respect she deserves as you leave our office!"

Jack Arms stands next to Shanette with his arm around her shoulders as he bows and waves his hand towards the elevator suggesting Dove leave now. Embarrassed, T'ondra rolls her eyes at Shanette and tells Scott to ask his friend how her pussy tasted after kissing him, then she stands with a smirk on her face as the doors close.

Chapter 13
Trouble Finds A Way

Scott and Shanette sat at a coffee shop on lunch break discussing the performance T'ondra put on in the office a few hours earlier. He told her about the relationship he had with her, or whatever they were to each other. Dove just mainly used him. When she was at a low point in her life he was there to lift her spirits with kind words and an attentive ear. By T'ondra being his celebrity crush and being physically attracted to her led to several sexual encounters. Shanette was taken aback by how honest he was being, but appreciated it.

"I guess if my celebrity crush came on to me, I may go weak for him too, but you must have put something fierce on her ass to make her go off the deep end like that chubbs!"

Scott laughed and told her no and that she must be drinking again for her to be that extra. "It's kind of sad, but there was no excuse for that shit."

"Yeah I know. It's not like we are actually seeing each other, we are just friends." Then she reached out and touched his hand.

Looking into her eyes he says yes, friends, very sadly. He then holds her hand and tells her that in their early college years he had always wanted to ask her out, but now that he was a grown man that fear was gone.

"Ms. Shanette Tolls, may I ask you to accompany me out on a date?"

"Mr. Mozell yes you may and I would be very happy to go on a date with you."

Then Scott's phone rang. He looked at the number and didn't recognize it at first. Searching his mind, he remembers it as Andrea's cell number. At first, he wasn't going to answer it, but she had done nothing to him. She told him that T'ondra had been going on drinking binges and she is doing real damage to herself. She had already fallen down the stairs and on another occasion, she fell in the pool drunk and almost drowned. Another person would not have given two shits about her, but Scott was very compassionate and sympathetic. Especially to those not in control of themselves. He tells her if he could help let him know, then he hung up.

"Now back to this date." Scott says as he gives Shanette his full attention.

"Scott, I have a confession. My heart isn't ready for another relationship right now. Although I wasn't with Anthony Regal long, we had a connection. Now we have always had a strong bond as friends, but I wouldn't want to ruin it trying to evolve it into a romance. "

"I can tell you are serious, because since we have reconnected you have called me chubbs. Now it's Scott. Shanette, I am also dealing with matters of the heart. I thought me and T'ondra had something, but I was hoping for love and she was playing with it. How about we just go out with no more expectations than Tolls and Mozell having a good time together."

"That sounds perfect chubbs."

The day has come, and Scott is rather excited about going out with Shanette. Sure, they have been out together before, but it was always with a group of friends. He even had the approval of Daryl who told him that they should have gone out as a couple way back in college. Scott tells his friend that the timing was completely wrong back then, but now after both of them experiencing heart destroying events, they need to lean on each other now.

Dressed, looking good, and smelling good, Scott gets ready to head out the door when who is standing in his driveway, but T'ondra Dove. Leaning on her car smiling, wearing a small track jacket and more than likely small shorts.

"T' why are you here? All the times I asked you over and you declined, now you show up after fucking someone right in my damn face! How dare you! Better yet get the hell away from here."

Not listening to him she stepped closer to him and opened her jacket exposing her naked body. Scott looked at her and his penis twitched, but his thinking head overruled. Telling her to close her jacket and go home before a neighbor came out and saw her. Although it was night, it wasn't truly dark yet. His date with Shanette was at 8. T'ondra rolled up on him at 7:15.

When she finally spoke, she stuttered, and her breath smelled like a broken bottle of whiskey. Reaching out for him she fell up against his chest and burped letting a small amount of vomit out. There go his clothes for the night and he still needed to get her away so he can go. He turned to go into the house to quickly change. T'ondra stumbled in the house behind him mumbling something about drinking was the only thing she could do to take his place in her life. The only other thing that comforted her. Grabbing a clean shirt out of his closet that went with his pants and shoes he rushed back through the house grabbing her arm to make her leave.

Coming out of his home with a drunk naked woman in tow he stopped and froze in place. Now standing midway in his driveway was Shanette, she was all smiles.

"Surprise! I thought I would surprise you by coming to pick you up since you are picking up the bill for dinner." Then her face changed after seeing him buttoning up his shirt and a naked woman following out behind him.

"Oh Scott. Your little young bitch is here now. Maybe she wants to kiss you and taste my pussy again!"

Shanette stepped back and looked at them. "You motherfucker! You were playing me…"

He cut her off trying to explain what was going on. Dove went past him and got in her face cussing and screaming. Opening her little jacket, she told Shanette that he had been doing her for the last hour and her cat was oh so sore. Shanette put her hand on

Doves face and pushed her to the ground. Shanette didn't even look at Scott, she just got in her car and left. On the ground T'ondra sat and laughed as she pulled away and Scott ran out in the street chasing her. Getting up she got in her own car and drove off through Scott's yard.

Chapter 14
I Never Knew

Daryl and Scott sat on the back of Scott's work truck sipping on a couple of cold drinks. They just finished the last project of the week and was talking about how glad that this was an easy job, so much easier than The Donovan Agency. Not because that job was hard, that job just had a lot of little details that needed to be perfect for that company. They also discussed what Scott went through with T'ondra Dove.

"Dude that chick may not be able to hold her liquor, but she has to have some deep feelings for you to act an ass like that."

"Man, the only feeling she may have for me is that she misses the attention and sex. Besides, I think me and Shanette could actually build something together. We've been friends for a long time."

Taking a swallow of the cold drink Daryl shakes his head in agreement then tells his buddy to think about it. "Shanette is cool people no doubt, but T'ondra is a damn star. Or used to be. The lifestyle you could have with her would be insane."

"That's true, but what about caring for each other?"

"Feelings would grow because there is something there as a basis. Dude you know how excited you were to be with your celebrity crush. You know what to do, just get your ass out of here and do it."

Daryl got up and gave Scott a bro hug and poured the rest of his drink out, got in his car and drove away smiling out the window. Scott did the same with his drink, closed the tailgate then hoped in the truck and drove off.

Scott finally got to his destination and jumped out the truck. He rehearsed what he would say all the way there. Going up to the door and ringing the bell he began to sweat.

Then the door open and that beautiful woman stood in front of him.

"Before you say anything please let me say this. I know that there is no romantic love between us, but I feel there could be if we both want it bad enough. I know it deep down inside and I feel you do too. Now I'm not saying it has to be right away, but damnit we need to give it a chance. I know your issues and you know mine so there are no secrets between us."

She gets ready to speak, but Mozell holds his hand up to keep her from doing it.

"From struggling with our things, we deserve to be happy, we deserve to be the one that makes the other happy." Then Scott got down on his knees and held her hands and begged her to give him, give them, give love a chance. "...PLEASE!!!! Can you please just try?"

"Get up off your knees. True, I said that we don't have a romantical tie, but seeing how passionate you are right now I can only imagine how you would treat me. Now before you get all starry-eyed, I'm only agreeing to think about giving it a try. I'm not sure yet, but before we even think about connecting like that what you going to do about that other chick?"

"You don't have to worry about her. That's over and done with...period. Daryl gave me some advice that I'm taking, he told me you know what to do so get up off your ass and do it. I'm here doing it."

"I'm not worried about that confrontation at the agency, but what about what went down at your house?"

"I didn't know she was coming over, that was a complete unwanted surprise. I want to apologize about that."

"So, you say!"

"That's true."

She walked out closer to him, then put her hand on his chest and smiled. "I know she wasn't supposed to be there. That strong ass smell of liquor on her breath almost knocked me down. Besides what kind of chick still rides around naked under jackets. You wanna be sexy take your things off in front of him and give him a show."

"Guess she is a star thot."

"Nah, she is a T.A.S!"

"What is a TAS?"

"A Trifling Ass Slut!"

They both laughed and hugged. He asked her if she was sure. Shanette said sure chubbs, we have been down a long time. We have a friendship love, and we're both single. So, we will see where this will go." They hugged again and shared their first kiss as more than friends. He told her finding a woman as good as her, was his true wildest dream.

Epilogue

Music was barring, people dancing and singing, having a great time. Club Chocolate Silk was jumping like always, but no one was having a better time than Scott Mozell and Shanette Tolls. They went out several times and each date better than the last. The feelings they had for each other as friends grew into something more, there was something they felt for one another in college, but the timing was never there. So, it was so easy for them to take the next step now.

T'ondra Dove had a new plaything now, a man she met in an A.A. meeting who happens to be a master chef. So, she no longer bothered Scott for attention or sex. That could be because she gave up trying to be a dramatic actress and hooked up with a company to design and sell a line of sex toys.

Shanette wasn't completely over Regal, but accepting his death was much easier with Scott's help and support.

While sitting at a table in a corner of the club at the bar area, Shanette looked towards the entrance and stared. Blinking repeatedly and rapidly she put her drink down and rubbed her eyes.

"You ok honey?"

"Yes. This drink must be too strong because it's got me seeing shit."

They laughed, then Shanette was about to take a sip of water when someone caught her attention again. She dropped the glass completely as her mouth flew open. He asked if she was sure she was alright when at that moment someone came up to their table.

"Pardon the intrusion, but I had to come over and speak. Hello Shanette! Oh, excuse me where are my manners. Hello sir. My name is…

Shanette spoke before him and said, "REGAL!!!" Then she fainted.

The End